# Homecoming

# Homecoming

## Diane Dakers

orca soundings

ORCA BOOK PUBLISHERS

**Library and Archives Canada Cataloguing in Publication**

Dakers, Diane, author
Homecoming / Diane Dakers.
(Orca soundings)

Issued in print and electronic formats.
ISBN 978-1-4598-0804-1 (bound).--ISBN 978-1-4598-0803-4 (pbk.).--
ISBN 978-1-4598-0805-8 (pdf).--ISBN 978-1-4598-0806-5 (epub)

I. Title.  II. Series: Orca soundings
PS8607.A43H64 2014          jC813'.6          C2014-901565-8
                    C2014-901566-6

First published in the United States, 2014
**Library of Congress Control Number:** 2014935387

**Summary:** When Fiona's dad is released from prison for a crime he says he did not
commit, Fiona struggles with whom to believe and how to move forward.

*Orca Book Publishers is dedicated to preserving the environment and has
printed this book on Forest Stewardship Council® certified paper.*

Orca Book Publishers gratefully acknowledges the support for its publishing
programs provided by the following agencies: the Government of Canada through
the Canada Book Fund and the Canada Council for the Arts,
and the Province of British Columbia through the BC Arts Council
and the Book Publishing Tax Credit.

Cover image by iStock

ORCA BOOK PUBLISHERS          ORCA BOOK PUBLISHERS
PO Box 5626, Stn. B          PO Box 468
Victoria, BC Canada          Custer, WA USA
V8R 6S4          98240-0468

www.orcabook.com
Printed and bound in Canada.

17  16  15  14  •  4  3  2  1

*For all the innocents.*

# Chapter One

I am so sick and tired of defending my dad. I'm sick of talking about *the incident*, tired of being hassled about it. I feel like getting Mr. Hazel to put it on the morning announcements. That way, everyone in the school will hear it all at once: "Attention all students: Fiona Gardener's father DID NOT TOUCH

THAT GIRL. The lying little drunken skank made it all up."

Well, I guess the principal wouldn't call Morgan a skank. But everyone knows what she is. And what she did. I still can't believe nobody called her out on it. Some sort of party code. What happens at a party-where-underage-kids-are-drinking stays at the party-where-underage-kids-are-drinking.

Anyway, I thought it was ancient history. I thought that everyone had finally gotten over the whole "Fiona's dad is a rapist" thing. Nobody has bugged me about it for months.

It was brutal when my dad was first charged. The whole school was talking about him and *that girl*. Thankfully, it got old pretty quick, and the haters soon moved on to the next poor schmo.

Of course, it all heated up again during his trial. And when he was convicted, I thought I would never hear the end of it—it was in the newspaper, after all. Luckily, it was just before summer vacation, so I could escape for a couple of months. Thank goodness we live out in the boonies, too far from town for the bullies to bother messing with me.

When my dad first went away, Mom and I, Uncle David and Aunt Helen, the neighbors—we were all pretty messed up about it. Nobody actually thought Dad would go to jail. After all, he didn't do it. At least I'm pretty sure he didn't do it. He's not like that.

But when that two-faced little stoner started crying in court, and her psycho mother ranted about how *that man* had ruined her darling little angel's life… well, the judge bought it, hook, line and sinker.

After the sentencing hearing that November, Mom kept me home from school for a few days. To protect me from the name-calling. And the questions. And the looks. And the whispers. And the rumors. And…and…and…

It didn't help though. It takes more than a few days for the creeps to get over it. No way they're going to let go of a chance to pick on someone like me. I'm such an easy target. Such a *nice* girl. Easy pickings for someone like Zak, the school's biggest butthole.

That was a long time ago, though, and everyone at school finally moved on. They forgot about the party, the police, the court case. Even Zak stopped harassing me. He moved on to target someone else a few weeks after my dad went away.

But now that my dad is coming home, it's all started up again. Why can't they all just leave me alone? It's not like *I* went to jail. It's not like *I* did anything wrong.

I kind of wish my dad wasn't coming home tonight. I mean, I miss him and everything. But having an ex-con for a father is going to make my life hell all over again.

## Chapter Two

It's long after dinner and Dad's still not here. Everyone is getting pretty antsy.

Mom's been totally wired since she got home from work today. Tidying everything in sight. Looking at her watch a thousand times. Checking her hair and makeup every ten minutes. She barely ate any supper.

She invited a bunch of people over to welcome Dad home. Simon and May are here. And Elisabeth from next door. They've all had some wine. Mom even gave me half a glass.

I wonder if I'll even recognize Dad. After all, it's been sixteen months and eight days since I last laid eyes on him.

Mom never let me go with her to visit him. "It's no place for a teenage girl," she said. Plus, it was far—a four-hour drive—so I would have had to miss a day of school if I'd gone with her. I talked to him on the phone a couple of times a week, but that was enough jail time for me, Mom said.

When Uncle David's car pulls up, we all head outside into the dark. Mom takes a deep breath—and another swig of her wine—before she joins us in the cold night air. She doesn't seem all that happy about Dad coming home.

She seems more edgy than excited. I hear her ask May to stick close, to not leave her alone with Dad for a little while.

When Dad and Uncle David get out of the car, they don't come up the walk right away. They unload a few things from the back seat. Dad puts his coat on and stops to tie his shoes. Uncle David goes into the garage to get some windshield washer fluid for the car. Everybody is acting so awkward.

Finally, Simon yells, "Hey, buddy, welcome home!" Simon is Dad's best friend. He walks toward the car and hugs Dad in one of those man-hugs, the kind where they pat each other on the back a few times. "About time you got here," says Simon, and everyone relaxes a little bit.

Elisabeth is next to hug Dad. She kisses him on the cheek and wipes a tear from her face with her mitten. "Good to see you, mister."

I'm in front of Mom and May, who are hanging back at the top of the stairs. That means I'm next in the receiving line. I can't really get out of it. Dad comes forward to hug me, but Honey steps between us, her way of telling him to keep his distance. She hasn't seen him for sixteen months and eight days either, and she isn't too sure about him. Dad reaches down and scratches her behind the ear. "How's my favorite pup?" he whispers. Honey, reassured and remembering, jumps on him, wags her tail and licks his face. As if nothing has changed. As if he's just come home after a long day's work. Traitor.

Then it's my turn. Dad's eyes are all teary. "I've missed you, Fiji." I let him hug me, but I sort of push him away at the same time. I don't want him to think I'm all that happy to see him. After all this time. After everything I've had to put up with while he's been away.

For the record, Dad's the only one who calls me Fiji. When I was little, people called me "FiFi." Which I hated. It's a baby name. Dad couldn't quite let it go though. So he started calling me "Fi G." Get it? Fiona Gardener. Fi G. Which eventually became Fiji. Like the island in the South Pacific Ocean. I used to like it that Dad had a special name for me.

Now that I'm practically an adult— I'm fifteen and a quarter—Mom calls me by my actual name, which makes me feel quite grown up. Even though my name means "fair" or "white" in Scottish, I think it's sort of a superhero-girl name. The kind of name that takes care of its owner. I'm the only Fiona I know, and I like that it sets me apart a little bit. I'm not Emily or Ashley or Jessica like so many of the girls at school.

My friends still call me by the little-kid names they've always called me.

To them, I'm still FiFi. Or Fi-Fy-Fo-Fum. Or Feenee-Swaheenee. No idea where that one came from, but Eric next door, Elisabeth's son, invented it. He still calls me that for some reason.

Some of the kids at school, the ones who don't know me that well, have been calling me other things lately. Convict-kid. Slammer-sister. Baby-jailbird. As if I was the one who was in prison.

I grab Honey by the collar and drag her out of the way so the others can say hello to Dad. So that I can get away from him.

May leaves Mom's side to greet him, keeping Mom and Dad apart for another few seconds. A hug and a kiss, and then it's Mom's turn. She and Dad don't look each other in the eye when they say hello. They don't really say much at all to each other before he hugs her in one of his big bear hugs. More tears. She looks the way

11

I feel—uncomfortable, confused, self-conscious about having this reunion in front of all these other people. They're Mom's best friends, but still…

The last time Mom saw Dad, he was wearing an orange jumpsuit, and he was behind a glass wall. She told me they'd had to talk to each other through a cracked telephone stained with the germs of all the visitors who'd been to see other inmates before her. The guards gave her a little moist towelette to wipe the phone with. But it couldn't wipe away Mom's disappointment with Dad.

"Enough with the happy reunion," yells Simon. "Let's get the hell inside. It's friggin' freezing out here!" What would we do without Simon?

In the house, Dad takes off his coat, and I notice that he's fatter than the last time I saw him. I suppose there's not much to do in jail. Just lots of sitting around waiting—and gaining weight. He looks kind of gray too, like he hasn't seen the sun for months. And he's jumpy. The phone rings—it's Grandma—and he almost pees himself. Totally freaks him out.

Simon and May and the others don't end up staying too long. I guess they want to give Mom and Dad and me a chance to get reacquainted.

Mom and I just go to bed though, leaving Dad lying on the couch. Honey is the only one getting a good night's sleep tonight.

## Chapter Three

Dad and a couple of his buddies are in the garage this morning. Male bonding over tools and car stuff, things that were neglected while Dad was away.

"The food was disgusting. The coffee was even worse. I had no privacy. Ever." Dad is telling the guys what it was like in jail. They don't realize I can hear them. I'm in the laundry room, which opens into the garage. I'm pretending to fold the clothes that were in the dryer. I have folded the same shirt ten times already.

"The guards were goons," Dad says. "They listened in on all our phone calls. They opened all our mail and read it before they gave it to us. Sometimes, they raided our cells just because they could. One time, I had a photo of Fiona and her mom on the wall. They pulled it down and tore it up."

I unfold the shirt and start again.

"Some days, they would let us outside for a few minutes. I didn't have a coat. But I would rather freeze outside than stay inside a minute longer than I had to. Otherwise, during our 'free' time, all sixteen of us were stuck together in one big room. It was always so loud. So many fights over the stupidest things. I just kept my head down and tried not to get beat up."

Poor Dad. No wonder he never wanted to say much on the phone. He always wanted to talk about me and school and Mom and Honey.

"Since when do you fold laundry, Fiona?" I jump. I didn't hear Mom sneaking up on me.

"I just thought I'd help you today," I tell her, trying to look innocent and making enough noise that she can't hear Dad talking. I don't want her to know I was eavesdropping.

"Well, thank you for your help. It looks like you're almost finished. When you're done with that last shirt, I'd like you to come grocery shopping with me."

"Mom, I hate grocery shopping. It's Saturday. It's my day off. Can't I stay home? I was going to make some bracelets and take Honey for a walk. I could do more laundry for you." I smile sweetly.

"Fiona, enough. I want you to come with me." Mom doesn't usually care whether I go shopping with her or not. Since I turned fifteen, she has let me stay home by myself a few times. Besides, Dad's here now, so what's the big deal? Not that I want to hang out with him. I just want to be left alone.

"Fiona, let's go. We can walk the dog when we come home. While we're out, we could stop at the craft store and get some new beads for your jewelry projects if you'd like."

I'll admit it. I can be bribed. We live so far out of town that, any time Mom offers to take me to the shops I like, I take her up on it. It's a half-hour drive just to the supermarket, and even farther to the shopping center. The only buses that come out here are school buses. And I'm not old enough to drive myself. So okay. I'll go grocery shopping if it means I can get some supplies to try out some of my new jewelry designs.

"Fine," I sigh. I pick up the laundry basket and stomp down the hall. I don't want Mom to think I'm happy about going with her.

As soon as we pull out of the driveway, I realize why Mom made me come along. She wants to *talk*. She wants to know how I'm *feeling* about Dad being home. Or maybe she wants to tell me how she's feeling. Either way…*gag*.

"Fiona, I know it's just been you and me for the past year and a half," she says. "And we did okay, didn't we? Two gals taking care of each other."

Yeah, sure, whatever.

"It's okay if you aren't sure how to act around him now," she says. "We've all been through a lot, and people change when they go through tough times. Your dad has changed. You and I have changed."

What is she on about? I know Mom was angry that Dad didn't fight harder to stay out of jail, and that she had to look after everything while he was away. He lost his job, and we almost lost the house. What is she trying to say?

"Are you going to get a divorce?" I blurt out.

"I don't know about that, Fiona. But things between your dad and me aren't going to be the same as they were before he went away. We have to get used to each other again. And you might not feel the same way toward him as you did before. I just want you to know that it's okay for you to feel whatever you're feeling."

Yeah, sure, whatever. What does she want me to say?

"Are you mad at him for going to jail?" she asks.

"I dunno. Maybe"

"Are you happy he's home?"

Sort of, but sort of not. I think it, but I don't say anything. I just look out the window. I don't want to talk about any of this.

"Fiona, are you afraid of your father now that he's been to jail?"

Whaaaaat? What I'm afraid of is this moment. Being trapped in a car with my mother asking me all kinds of stupid questions.

"You know your father didn't do what he was accused of doing, don't you?"

"Mom. Stop it!" I yell at her. "I don't want to be having this conversation. Dad is just Dad. All I know is that my life has been hell because of him. I don't get a moment of peace at school. Can't I at least have that at home? Why can't everyone just leave me alone about this? He's home. It's over. Let's just get back to normal now. *Okay*?"

For the next two hours, Mom and I don't say much. We shop. We buy groceries. I buy lots of crafty stuff. She's feeling guilty for bugging me, so she lets

me buy pretty much anything I want—
beads and charms, a book of jewelry
designs, even a few new tools.

When we get home, we still don't
say much. But she still won't leave me
alone. She comes with me on my walk
with Honey. She never comes with me
when I walk the dog. "I need some
fresh air," she tells Dad. Otherwise,
she doesn't say much to him either.

## Chapter Four

I'm not sure which is worse—spending the weekend at home with my parents, or going back to school today.

The whole weekend was pretty tense. Dad worked hard at being jolly, trying to turn back the clock to life before *the party*, Mom barely speaking to him, lots of people dropping by to see him after all this time. Everyone wants to know,

"What was it like in jail?" Can't they see he just wants to forget it ever happened? We all do. Move on, people.

But now it's Monday, and I know it won't be the best day of my life. I caught a break because Dad came home on Friday night, so I had a couple of days away from the trash-talking at school. But I figure there's a big target on my forehead today.

I always wait for the school bus with Eric, Kelsey and Tay, my next-door neighbors. Tay, whose real name is Taylor, is my best friend in the neighborhood. We're both in grade ten, and we have some classes together. Mostly, though, we hang out after school and on the weekends. She has a dog too, so we walk them in the woods together, and take them to the beach in the summer. Rocky and Honey give us a good excuse to get out of the house, away from parents breathing down our necks.

This is Kelsey's first year taking the bus with us. She's only fourteen, in grade nine, but she's already tougher than me and Tay. She's always being grounded for something or other. Not that Kelsey ever learns from it. As soon as she's allowed out of the house again, she's off to some meet-up with the party girls, the ones who smoke pot and think nobody knows about it. The ones who wear skin-tight tops to show off for the horny boys. The ones who dye their hair until it's bleach-blond trampy. I hate to say it, but I don't actually like Kelsey all that much. She's Tay's sister though, so I never say anything bad about her.

Eric on the other hand—he's pretty awesome. He's in grade twelve, so he's going to grad in a couple of months. It will be weird getting on the bus without him next year. He's always been there with us, sort of looking out for me and Tay—and now Kelsey—in a big-brother kind of way. He's never in our faces about it, but we know he has our backs.

Today, when the bus pulls up, we can already hear Zak being loud and ugly. Of course, as soon as we climb aboard, he starts in on me. "Hey, jail-baby. I hear your jailbird dad is now an ex-con. Better be careful he doesn't get his hands on you."

His loser friends get into the act too. "I bet your daddy was somebody's bitch in the big house," laughs Evan. Josh comes up with this brilliant rhyme: "Fi-Fy-Fo-Fum, FiFi's dad is prison scum."

Tay and I slide into seats near the front of the bus, as far from these morons as we can get. Kelsey hops down the aisle to sit with girls who giggle every time Zak opens his mouth. Eric follows Kelsey but stops at Zak's seat. He stares down my tormentor. "Shut it, douche bag," he says quietly. Then he sits down right behind Zak and Evan.

That's the great thing about Eric. He's a really nice guy, athletic, hand-some, smart and all that. But he's also that guy that other guys listen to. For some reason, they all want to please him. Or maybe they want to be him. Either way, once Eric tells them to, Zak and his groupies leave me alone. At least they leave me alone on the way to school.

Once we're there though, I can't escape them. But it's no longer just those guys. This morning, every classroom I walk into goes silent. Then some of the kids start whispering to each other, looking at me and giggling. Others just stare at me, then look away when I go to meet their eyes. I feel like I've just walked into class naked or something. Something dirty.

As if Mondays aren't bad enough, my first class of the day is math.

I actually like math, and I'm good at it. But it's so boring because Ms. Gaertner has to go so slowly, so the other dopes can keep up. At least I won't have to think too much just yet.

When I sit down, I see a piece of paper on my desk. I open it and read: *Now that your dad is home, you better sleep with the lights on, Fifi. Since Morgan left town, he'll be looking for another playmate.*

Don't react. Don't react. Don't react. I don't want whoever left this note to think it bugs me. I can feel my face turning red. I hear someone snuffling, like they're trying not to laugh. I look up quickly, hoping to catch someone in the act, someone looking my way or laughing. But everyone is staring straight ahead.

Right at that moment, Ms. Gaertner starts talking. "Okay, everyone. Last week, some of us were having trouble solving quadratic equations, so let's review some of the problems again."

At least while she's droning on, nobody's bothering me. Lauren passes me a note. *RU OK*? I shrug at her and nod, grateful that somebody is on my side. Lauren is a bit of a nerdy girl, but I like her. She's sweet. She comes over to my house sometimes to study, or to swim in the summer. She likes making jewelry too, so we've been working together on a collection. When we have enough pieces ready, we're going to sell them on one of those crafty websites. I'm pretty excited about that. Thinking about it helps me get through math class.

Lauren and I are in the same homeroom, so after math we walk together.

"I have to tell you something," she says as we push through crowds of kids. "My mom says that now that your dad is home, I'm not allowed to go to your house ever again."

I stop cold. "What?" is all I can manage to say.

"I told her that's stupid, that your dad is a good guy, that he didn't do anything to ugly Morgan. I told her that Morgan is an alcoholic, and you can't believe a word she says. I told her that everybody knows Morgan made it up. I said it was your dad's word against hers—and the stupid judge believed her."

Lauren is talking a mile a minute.

"I'm really sorry, Fiona. I want to keep coming to your place. But my mom thinks I should stay away. 'Just in case,' she says. Even though she knows your dad. Even though she knows Morgan is a lying freak."

She stops. "I'm really sorry," she says again.

I can't believe what I'm hearing. Now one of my friends isn't allowed to come to my house because of my dad? I wonder who else is going to break this kind of news to me today. I don't know what to say. So I don't say anything. I just keep my head down and go to my desk.

After homeroom, my teacher, Ms. Yung, asks me to stay back for a few minutes.

What now, I wonder.

"Fiona, I heard that your dad came home from…Well, I know your father was away, and he came home on Friday."

I stare at her. She's being all awkward. Everybody is being so weird right now. *Spit it out*, I want to yell at her.

"Fiona, what I'm trying to say is, if you ever feel, you know, unsafe at your house, you can tell me. Okay? I don't want you to feel you have to go home after school if your dad…I mean, if your mom isn't home from work yet. You can do homework here, and we can phone her, and she can pick you up on her way home. Okay?"

"Umm. Sure," I say. But really I want to scream.

This is the worst day of my life.

# Chapter Five

Luckily, nobody gives me any grief on the way to my next class. I'm a bit late because of Buttinsky-Yung, so the halls are pretty quiet. I guess I should thank her for that.

Just as I'm bracing myself to enter the classroom though, Ms. Shama comes out and nabs me. She was waiting inside, waiting to pounce on me. She steers me back into the hallway. "Fiona, I'd like to have a word with you, if I may. Let's go to my office."

This can't be good. Ms. Shama is the school social worker.

"But I'll miss French class," I protest.

"It won't take long, and Madame Pierre knows you're with me." Sheesh. Nice to know these teachers have my life all worked out. I feel like I have no say in anything today.

"It's up to you, Fiona," she says. Is she reading my mind now too? "I'm not going to force you to come with me, but I have some information I'd like to share with you."

I look into the classroom and see Zak and Evan's creepy faces sneering in my direction. Like they're just waiting to hurl more crap at me. Like they've searched online to find all kinds of ways to insult me *en français*, and they can't wait to try them out. It might actually improve their marks—that would be the closest thing to French homework they've ever done!

The thought of dealing with them right now makes my stomach turn. Maybe talking to Ms. Shama isn't such a bad idea. "Okay," I tell her and follow her down the hall.

She chitchats all the way to her office. "Isn't it a nice day," she chirps. "Spring is in the air. I saw some flowers budding in my garden this morning. And the robins have come back. A sure sign of spring."

I tune her out. She's always so peppy. I guess that's part of the job—she deals with kids in trouble all day long, so she must have to work hard to convince them that life really isn't so bad. Right now, I'm happy to put up with perky if it gets me away from obnoxious Zak and his followers.

When we get to her office, Ms. Shama offers me tea, water, juice. I decline. "Call me Maria," she says, like she's my new BFF. Then she gets to the point.

"Fiona, I know your father has been in prison, and I know why he was there. I also know he came home on Friday evening."

Here we go.

Over the next half hour, she talks about "staying safe," about letting adults know how I'm feeling, about services that are available to "kids in your situation." She hands me pamphlets and phone numbers, a list of websites, even her cell phone number. "If you feel scared or threatened, call me, or go to a neighbor's house, or call nine-one-one if you have to." Perky Shama has morphed into Serious Shama.

"How are you feeling right now?" she finally asks.

I feel like throwing up. I am so sick of all this. If it's not the haters nagging me, it's the teachers worrying about me, and now Ms. Shama, I mean *Maria*, is trying to save me from my criminal father.

"I'd like to go back to French class," I announce. That's all I have to say, and there's not much she can do but let me go. She did say it was up to me whether I talk to her or not.

In reality, it's almost time for my lunch period, so instead of going back to French, I head to the cafeteria. It's still full of students from first lunch, and I see Tay in there. We almost never get lunch together, so I make a beeline for her. She's sitting with a few other girls I know. Friends.

As soon as I get to the table, though, the questions start. These girls know the story. They know Morgan was bad news, and they know my dad didn't touch her.

They're nice girls, and I like them. But they're curious, just like everyone else.

"Did your dad get beat up in jail?" "What's it like seeing him again?" "Has he said anything about Morgan?" "Does your mom still love him?" "Is he allowed to be alone with you?"

No. Fine. No. I think so. Yes.

Questions, questions, questions.

The bell rings to signal that first lunch period is over and mine is just beginning. Saved by the bell, I think to myself.

As they leave and the caf empties, I have a few minutes to myself—the first bit of peace I've had all day. When the next group starts filing in, I realize I can't face what I know is coming. Lunchtime is a free-for-all at the best of times, but today will be a nightmare for me. Zak and his cronies—and everyone else who has an opinion on my life, my dad, my home, my safety—will be in my face about it.

I grab my knapsack and get out of there before anyone sees me. I find Madame Pierre and tell her *je suis malade*. I have to miss the second half of French class, and I need to go home. I'm not sure how to say "I'm gonna throw up" in French, but it doesn't matter. Madame understands. She tells me to go to the school office and wait for a ride. That's the protocol.

I phone my mom to pick me up, but she's in a meeting. I try Elisabeth— she's been Mom's backup for the past year and a half. Not home.

Normally, I'd have to sit and wait for one of them to come for me, but then I remember my dad. He's at home now. School protocol can't stop me from asking my own father to come pick me up. He says he'll be right over.

# Chapter Six

When Dad arrives, I yell "bye" to the office staff and dash outside. I don't want him to come in, or even get out of the car. I don't want anyone to see him. I don't want to give anyone anything more to gossip about. I can only imagine what kind of barf they'd make up if they knew I was going home *alone* with my felon of a father.

I get to the car before he's even parked it. When I jump in, it's all I can do not to shout, "Go, go, go!" As if we're bank robbers making a fast getaway before the cops arrive.

As soon as we're on the road, I realize this is the first time I've been alone with my dad since he came home. Mom hasn't left us alone together at all. What's up with that?

Does she not trust him around me anymore? Does that mean she thinks maybe he is guilty of what Morgan accused him of? Obviously a lot of people think so. Otherwise, why would Ms. Shama—no way I can call her *Maria*—and Ms. Yung be acting all weird and protective of me? Why would Lauren's mother not let her come to my house anymore? Should I be afraid of my own father?

"Are you feeling any better now?" Dad interrupts my racing brain.

"Huh? Yeah, I guess." I'm not in the mood to talk. Especially not to him. After all, it's because of him that my life has become such a disaster.

Dad is quieter these days than he used to be. He hasn't really said much since he came home. But right now, in the car, he's trying to be all buddy-buddy with me.

"How were your first couple of classes this morning?"

"Fine."

This is going to be the longest twenty-minute drive of my life.

"Do you still feel like throwing up?"

"Nope."

We drive in silence for a few minutes. I stare out the window. Ms. Shama is right. It *is* a nice day out. Then Dad wrecks it.

"Fiji, did anything happen at school this morning to make you feel bad?"

I sigh, but I don't respond.

"I mean, you seemed fine when you left this morning."

I shrug but still say nothing. *Let it go, Dad. Let it go. Everyone else is in my face. All because of you. Don't make it worse.*

"Did anyone say anything to…"

"Yes, Dad. Yes, something happened to make me feel bad. Yes, someone said something to upset me. What do you think? My dad is a jailbird. A con. Now an ex-con. He's a rapist. He's a criminal. I'd better watch my back or else I'll be my dad's next victim. My friends aren't allowed to come over anymore. The whole school is having a field day. And the teachers think you're going to attack me or something. Even Mom…"

I stop talking.

"Even Mom what, Fiji?"

"Nothing. Never mind."

"What were you going to say, Fiona?" He never calls me Fiona.

42

Tears start to sting my eyes. I can't speak. I shake my head and turn to the window. I focus on what a very-nice-day it is out there.

A few minutes pass. "I'm sorry, Fiji. I know this whole thing has been hard on you. I wish none of this had happened. If I could turn back time and have one do-over in my life, I would go back to the night of that party and do things differently. I wouldn't agree to chaperone without any other adults present. I would have said no when Uncle David asked me to help him out."

"But you didn't," I cry. "You went. And who knows what happened there. Something must have happened, or else you wouldn't have gone to jail. Why did you go there that night? Why did you do it? Why did you do this to me?"

The floodgates are open now, and I can't stop myself. "Do you have any idea what my life has been like since the night of that party? The trash-talking. The questions. The rumors. The whispers. The looks. I've become the girl-whose-father-is-in-jail. I'm always defending you, and I'm tired of it. I don't even know what is true anymore. Maybe you are what they say you are."

I pause to take a breath. I hear my dad sniff. Is he crying? For Pete's sake, this is all his fault. What is he crying about?

"I'm just tired of all the adults asking me how I *feel,* and all the kids at school treating me like I'm some sort of freak," I say. "I haven't done anything to deserve this." I'm running out of steam now. I just want out of the car.

Finally Dad opens his mouth. "You're right, Fiji. You don't deserve this. I am so sorry for everything I've put you through."

Finally, we are pulling into the driveway. Finally, this car ride from hell is over. "Things aren't always what they seem," Dad sighs as he puts the car in Park. "Things aren't always black-and-white."

The car has barely stopped when I open the door and escape into the house. I drop my knapsack, grab Honey and her leash and run back outside and down the driveway. "I'm taking the dog for a walk," I yell as I head for the woods.

## Chapter Seven

Once we get to the woods, I stop running. It isn't too far from our house, but today it feels like it isn't far enough.

What I call "the woods" is actually a huge forest reserve. Mom says that means it will always be here. Nobody will ever be allowed to chop down the trees and build roads or houses.

You can walk for miles and miles and hardly ever see another person. In fact, it would be really easy to get lost in these woods. I come here so often, though, that I know every path and tiny trail. I never get lost—unless I want to not be found.

Today, I feel like getting lost and never going home.

In the winter, people come here to cross-country ski. In the summer, the ski trails become hiking trails. Right now, it's that mucky, early-spring, in-between state, so it's even emptier than usual. Which suits me just fine.

I let Honey off her leash, so she can explore. There are so many good smells in here for a hound. She always follows her nose, tracking deer, or raccoons, or porcupines. She's in doggie heaven!

Pretty soon, the partiers will come back. When the weather's nice, they come in here to build bonfires, to drink, smoke pot, eat junk food and waste time. They're such dolts, they think nobody knows they're here. Like the forest is their big, secret, personal party palace.

It won't be long before we start finding beer cans and cooler bottles, potato chip bags and candy wrappers again. Sometimes when we walk the dogs, Tay and I bring garbage bags with us. We hate cleaning up after those pigs, but we don't want the woods to become a big garbage dump.

One time, years ago, before I was even born, one particularly dumbass group of partiers left a fire going and burnt down a big chunk of the woods. The community association replanted the trees, perfectly even rows of evergreens with no low branches—leaving nowhere to hide. After all these years, though, the poplars, maples, oaks and elms are finally filling in, so it's a bit more forest-like out here. It's a place that keeps secrets again. It's a place that just lets me be.

Right now, my mind is racing. How can I ever face school again? Maybe I should go live with Grandma for a while to get away from everything and everyone. What did Dad mean that everything isn't black-and-white? What are all my teachers so worried about? What do they think Dad is going to do to me? I wonder what I'm missing in the rest of my classes today. I wonder if my mom still loves my dad. Are they going to split up? What will happen to me then? How long can I stay in the woods before anyone comes looking for me?

I'm so deep in thought that I don't even see Charley until I'm almost on top of her. She's leaning against a tree, just off the path I'm walking on. She's drinking beer out of a can and patting Honey on the head.

Charley is in grade twelve. She's a good friend of my cousin Amy. They run with a hard-core crowd, way out of my league. Charley was at Amy's party that night two and a half years ago, the night Morgan accused my dad of…

"Hey," says Charley. I jump. I admit it, I've always been a bit afraid of Charley—and now here she is right in front of me. Actually talking to me. "You're Amy's cousin, right? Fiona."

"Ummm, yeah," I stutter.

"You skipping classes today too?"

I decide to play it cool. "Yeah," I answer. "I took off at lunchtime, halfway through French. You?"

"I didn't even bother going in today," she says. "I like your dog. What's his name?"

"It's a her, and it's Honey."

Charley snorts. "Honey. Ha. That's *sweet*." As if I've never heard that one before. By this time, Honey has wandered off a little, so I call her back. She comes right away and sits down beside me.

"How did you teach her to do that?" Charley asks.

"I dunno. She's always been a good dog. My dad spent a lot of time training her when we first got her."

"Your dad." Charley takes a sip of her beer. "I hear he came home on the weekend."

I brace myself for what's coming next. Of all people, I'm sure Charley has something to say about my dad, what happened that night, what other criminals did to him in prison, what he's going to do to me now that he's out of jail. She puts down her beer can, pulls out a package of cigarettes and lights one.

"Want a puff?" she asks, holding the smoke out to me. What, no snarky comments? No prison talk? No sniping?

"No thanks," I say. "But make sure you put it out when you're done." What am I, her mother? *Shut up, Fiona*, I tell myself, knowing I've just blown my cool-cover. I'm such a loser sometimes.

"Right." She nods. "The fire. It would suck if that happened again. Just when the forest is getting back to normal."

Maybe Charley isn't so scary after all. Maybe she's got a nice streak under that hoodie. She's the first person all day who hasn't grilled me about my dad. The first person to just let the subject go. Plus, Honey likes her. That's a good sign.

"You should come to a party with me and Amy one of these days," she says out of the blue. "You wouldn't be able to bring your dog though…Honey." She snickers when she says the name.

"Sure. Maybe. That sounds good," I say, amazed that this girl, one of the most badass kids in school, is actually inviting me—Goody Two-shoes Fiona— to a party. It'll probably never happen, but I'm honored in a weird way that she even said that to me.

Suddenly, Honey's ears perk up and she takes off after something. It gives me an excuse to move on. What I'm thinking is, even though my dad has ruined my life, he's probably worried about me, and I should get home.

What I say out loud is, "I'd better go after my dog. She doesn't listen so well when she's on the trail of something. So…ummm…bye. It's been nice talking to you."

*Nice talking to you*. I'm such a dork sometimes.

# Chapter Eight

I stayed home from school on Tuesday, but Mom and Dad made me go back on Wednesday. The bugging began on the bus, as usual, and continued for part of the day. At least the teachers had said all they had to say by then, so it wasn't quite so bad as Monday had been.

In the afternoon, though, a bizarre thing happened. A bunch of cop cars pulled up to the school. My stomach was instantly in my throat. Ever since my dad got arrested, I throw a panic every time I see a cop car. This time, I figured one of my ratty teachers had called them. I thought they had come to pick me up, to make sure I didn't go home ever again, to take me off to foster care, away from my criminal father.

I closed my eyes, and focused on deep breathing. My mom taught me to do this whenever I felt myself starting to freak out. In. Out. In. Out. Think peaceful thoughts.

Meanwhile, all my classmates had run to the window to watch the excitement. Even our history teacher was looking out, trying to figure out what was going on. Then an announcement over the PA system: "Attention all students and teachers," said Mr. Hazel in his most serious voice. "Please stay calm and stay in your classrooms. We have a problem, and the police are here. Please follow their instructions."

Maybe this had nothing to do with me after all. I started to relax—despite the fact that the SWAT team was swarming the school. Before long, two police officers came to our classroom door. They led us out of the room, out of the building and into the parking lot. They told us to stay put and stay together.

It was only two o'clock, but school buses started pulling up to take us home, to evacuate the school. Nobody had any idea what was going on. It wasn't until I got home and went online that I found out what had happened. It was all over the news sites. Everyone was talking about it.

It turns out that three grade-twelve girls—Jana, Bronwyn and Raiji—had planted a bomb in our school auditorium. Or at least they said they did. There was no explosion, and nobody was hurt, but the girls had been arrested. Crazy.

I was up half the night texting with Tay and Lauren about it.

Yesterday, it was all anybody talked about. Which was good for me.

Today, the cops are back at school, asking a lot of questions. They want to know more about the bomb girls. They want to know if anyone saw anything unusual on Wednesday. Nobody can— or will—tell them much. Funny how nobody knows anything when the police are around, but as soon as they're gone, everybody knows everything.

All I know is that the three wannabe bombers are friends of Amy and Charley, and everyone knows they're bad news. I was always surprised that Amy even hung out with them. She's tough, but she's not in their league of thugliness.

When the cops finally get around to interrogating the grade tens—they start with the twelves and work their way down the food chain—I tell them I don't know these girls at all. I don't tell them they might want to ask my cousin a thing or two.

In homeroom, Ms. Yung gives us a speech about being loyal to the school, not to students who want to hurt us. She talks about watching out for each other. She reminds us that Ms. Shama, my BFF Maria, is available if anyone wants to talk about their *feelings* about the bomb girls or the bomb scare or any other bombshells for that matter. Why do adults always want to talk about our *feelings*? Puke.

All we want to talk about is what happened on Wednesday. What were those girls thinking? Did they actually plant a bomb, or did they just want to prove that they could disrupt the school? Will they go to jail or just get a warning? Will they ever come back to school? Will they end up in juvie hall?

All I really care about is that nobody is talking about me anymore. Even on the bus on the way home, Zak, Evan and Josh ignore me. They're pretty impressed with the bomb girls, so they're trying to figure out ways to get into their pants. As if. Their talk gets pretty loud and raunchy, but I manage to tune it out.

The good news is that my life is no longer the hot topic of conversation. This Friday is already way better than last Friday was, and I have a feeling that this whole weekend is going to be an improvement over last weekend. Case closed on Fiona and her dad. The smack-talkers have left the building.

## Chapter Nine

I wake up Saturday morning to the sounds of Mom and Dad crabbing at each other. Again.

"What's that supposed to mean?" I hear Dad ask.

"Forget it," says Mom. "I'll deal with it later." I try to tune them out.

It's been like this ever since Dad came home. My parents weren't particularly lovey-dovey before Dad went away, but since he's been back, it's even worse.

I'm not sure they even *like* each other anymore. They think I can't hear them, that I don't know what's going on. I roll over and pull the covers over my head, wishing I couldn't hear them. And I don't even *want* to know what they're going on about this time.

What I do know is that Mom is really choked that Dad was so naïve about going to prison. He wasn't guilty, so he didn't hire a proper lawyer. Mom said he should have paid whatever it cost to hire the best lawyer in the city because in the end, he lost everything—his job, his friends, his freedom—trying to save a few bucks. "Being innocent doesn't keep you out of jail," she said. "A good lawyer does."

Ever since Dad's been home, Mom has been holding this I-told-you-so attitude over his head. I don't really blame her. Life sucked for both of us while Dad was away.

At first, it was really brutal. Nosy neighbors telling Mom she should get a divorce. Creepy emails to both of us from Morgan and her psycho mother—the cops took care of that pretty quick. And of course all the hassles I had at school.

We also had to cut back on everything to try and save money. No new clothes. Bag lunches only. No unnecessary car trips to the city. Even Honey had to switch to cheaper dog food.

Eventually, though, Mom and I found our groove. We got into a new routine. We figured out how to live with less, how to look after everything on our own—the house, the car, the pool. I guess what we really figured out was how to live our lives without Dad.

We got pretty good at it too. We basically started over. Our "new normal,"

Mom called it. But this new life didn't have Dad in it, so now that he's back, it's all messed up again. I mean I'm happy he's home and all, but it sucks all over again.

I can still hear them slamming around in the kitchen, so I get out of bed, knowing that when they see me, they'll stop griping at each other.

"Good morning, sweetie," Mom says as I wander into the kitchen. As if everything is fine, like we're living in an episode of *Leave It to Beaver*, that perfect-family, black-and-white TV show from a hundred years ago. "What would you like for breakfast this morning?" One big happy family!

After we eat, I do my usual Saturday morning chores. This is one part of the "new normal" I don't like—I have to do a lot more work around the house. I'm hoping now that Dad is back, my chore list will shrink. If Dad feels guilty enough,

I bet he'll sort the recycling for me, and tidy up all the coats and boots and dog stuff in the mudroom!

After we do our chores and shopping—Mom makes me go with her again—I text Tay to see if she and Rocky want to go for a walk with me and Honey. She says they'll be right over. That usually means about ten minutes, by the time she gets dressed and walks over here.

Even though we're next-door neighbors, our houses are quite far apart. We have so much space out here. That's the good thing about living outside the city. It's far away from all the shops and movies and everything, but we have a lot of room to roam, and our parents give us way more freedom than city kids have.

By the time Tay and Rocky arrive, Honey and I are ready to go. It's a gorgeous spring day, but we still have

to wear boots because of the muck.
I know, too, that when we get home,
I'll have to hose Honey down. She'll be
covered in mud.

The dogs start playing as soon as
they see each other. They sniff and jump
all over each other. They are as good
friends as Tay and I are.

I haven't spent as much time as usual
with Tay this week though. What with
being off school "sick," then the bomb
scare and all, it's been a chaotic few days.

We have a lot of catching up to do.
As we wander through the woods, we
mostly talk about my dad, what it's
been like this week with him home,
what he's said about being in jail. Tay
is the one person I can just talk to.
I don't have to defend myself or my
dad. No matter what anybody else at
schools says, we both *know* Morgan
framed him. Really, all the girls who
were at the party that night framed him

with their cone of silence. Including Amy and Charley. Why didn't they speak up to save my dad? Unless he really did do something wrong.

What I don't say out loud to Tay, what I've never said to anyone, is that I go over and over it all in my head— what my dad said happened that night, what Morgan said happened, what we know about Morgan's messed up life. I just wish I knew 100 percent for sure that my dad did not touch her. But I wasn't there. Nobody was. That's the problem. Just her and him upstairs while the other girls were downstairs.

Suddenly, Rocky starts yapping. Honey's back goes up, she slows down and focuses ahead and to the right. Tay and I have walked farther than usual, on a different path than usual. We've been so busy catching up that we haven't been paying attention to where we are.

We follow the dogs' focus. Argh. There's Zak and his buddies huddled around a little fire, drinking beer. We should have been watching where we were going.

"Hey, jail-baby," Zak shouts. Then he throws an empty can at Honey. She growls. "Wanna beer?"

I call Honey, and Tay grabs Rocky. We turn around, toward home.

"Oh, right, you don't need to get your beer from me, do you? Your dad gives it to you. He gives it to all the girls. So he can have his way with them…"

Then I hear a girl's voice. "Zak, you idiot, leave the dog alone." It's Charley. I didn't see her there. She nods my way, then flicks her head to the side, telling us to get lost. She has given me and Tay the break we need to get out of there before any trouble starts.

## Chapter Ten

For the rest of that weekend, and the next and the next, things are so tense between Mom and Dad that I'm actually relieved to go to school.

Nobody hassles me there anymore. Not as much, anyway. Zak and his pinhead friends still do a bit, but it turns out that morons have short memories. They've mostly moved on to new victims—kids with too many zits, bad haircuts or newly divorced parents.

Lauren is still not allowed to come to my house. That bugs me. I see her at school, but that's all. It means I'm pretty much on my own when it comes to our jewelry-making business. I haven't created much lately anyway. Now that the weather's nice, I just want to be outside, out of the house, away from all the bickering between Mom and Dad.

At school, though, I have to say it's been pretty smooth sailing. Maybe I'm finally waking up from the nightmare that has been my life for the past two years.

One morning, on my way to French, I run into Charley in the hallway. I've seen her around a bit, but I haven't talked to her since that day in the woods. "Hey, there's a party this weekend," she says. "You should come. Saturday."

I didn't think she'd actually remember her idea about me partying with her and Amy. And I don't actually think it's a very good idea. After all, I'm only fifteen, way under the legal drinking age, and these parties are all about getting drunk. Plus, the kids who go to these parties are not exactly my crowd.

At the same time, I don't want Charley to think I'm a total drip. She's one of the coolest kids at school, and she seems to think I'm cool too.

"Um, okay," I tell her, thinking I can jam out later and blame my parents.

"Great, I'll get Amy to text you with the deets." She dashes off. Probably needs a smoke before her next class.

On the bus on the way home, I tell Tay and Eric about Charley's invitation.

"Where's the party?" asks Eric.

"I dunno yet. Amy's going to text me."

"Who else will be there?"

"Who are you? My dad?" I tease him.

"Listen, Feenee-Swaheenee," he says in his most big-brotherly voice, "I'm just looking out for you, just like I would for Tay or Kelsey. I take care of all my kid sisters."

Hmmm. Kid sister. Why does it burn me so much that he considers me one of his kid sisters?

"Tell you what," he says. "Why don't I come with you? We can party together. Plus, if I don't go, there's no way you're going. No way, no how are your parents letting you go out on your own on a Saturday night."

Well, I wasn't going to tell them. But okay, I'd love for Eric to be my date for the night. He's one of those guys everyone is happy to have at a party. Charming, popular, nice to look at. All the girls are totally crushing on him. And all the guys fall all over themselves trying to be his best friend, trailing behind him like lost puppies, hoping to pick up some of the girls he leaves behind. Eric knows he can crash any party any time.

So it's settled. Eric and I are going to a party.

On Friday, Amy texts me the address. **C U 2moro**! she adds. I wonder if she really wants me there, or if she's doing what Charley tells her to do. Doesn't matter. I'm going. With Eric.

The party is at Jana's house. She's one of the bomb girls. None of them went to jail, by the way. Because they're under eighteen, they got off with a warning. I heard there was no bomb. They were just playing a joke. They wanted the teachers to know they could shut down the school any time they felt like it. Next time, the cops told them, they won't get off so easily.

Before I know it, it's Saturday night and I'm walking into the party.

I'm nervous, but knowing I'm with Eric helps. He was right though. The only reason my parents let me out of the house tonight is because he came with me. He drove me here and promised to bring me home at a reasonable time. Mom and Dad don't know Amy and her friends are here. No way they'd let me come if they knew that.

It's only eight o'clock when we arrive, but the house is packed. I see Charley and Amy across the room, hovering around Jana and the other bomb girls. Then, ugh, I see Zak and his gang. Eric steers me right up to them, and right past them. His eyes are locked on Zak's the whole time. Challenging him. Daring him to say anything mean to me. Zak keeps his trap shut. He and the other guys leave me alone because I'm with Eric.

A group of girls swarm us—because I'm with Eric. "FiFi, so glad you're here," they gush. What they really mean is, "Eric, we're so glad you're here. Why don't you ditch this little twerp and hang with us?" Do they really *not* know how obvious they are?

Eric and I keep moving. Everyone is drinking. Next thing I know, there's a beer in Eric's hand and a vodka cooler in mine.

It's not the first time I've had alcohol—Mom lets me have a small glass of wine now and again, now that I'm fifteen. But this is the first time I've had anything other than wine, and the first time I've ever had a drink outside my own house.

The cooler is pretty good. It's all pink and sweet and fizzy like pop. It has a bitter aftertaste, but I like it. It goes down easily. And quickly.

After I drink down the last swallow, I look at the beer in Eric's hand. It's only down about a quarter of the bottle.

He's been chatting so much with all the girls swooning over him that he's barely had a sip of his beer.

*Gag.* Why can't they just leave him alone? I can't watch this pathetic display for one more second. "I'm going to find Amy and Charley," I yell over the loud bass beat. He nods, and I wander away.

Amy and Charley are still with the bomb girls. I'm not brave enough to bust into that group, so I veer off toward the beer-and-cooler cooler instead. I pull out another bottle—orange this time. I twist off the top and take a swig. Hmm. Peach. Just as good as the pink one. As I sip, I look around. Of course I don't know anybody other than Amy, Charley and Eric. And Zak, who is keeping his distance. Thank you, Eric.

I find a place at the side of the room, where I can hover in the shadows by myself and watch the dancing and drinking. Eventually, though, Charley tracks me down. "Hey, you made it," she says, taking a mouthful of beer. "You should come meet Jana. It's her house, and you're drinking her pop."

"Oh, I thought it was for everyone," I stammer, embarrassed.

"It is, but you should at least say thank you." I follow Charley to where Amy and the bomb girls are standing. They're not talking to each other. Just looking around, glassy-eyed, swaying to the music. Amy throws her arms around me when she sees me.

"Fi-Fy-Fo-Fum, my favorite cousin has arrived…ba-dum." She laughs hysterically. "I made a rhyme for you," she shrieks.

"Good one," I say with a giggle. I pry myself from her grip.

"FiFi, these are my good friends Jana, Bronwyn and Raiji," she says, pointing. Then she points at me and speaks to them. "This is my cousin FiFi."

"Hi," I say to them. "Fiona. Nice to meet you. Thank you for inviting me to your party, Jana. And thanks for the coolers."

"No problem," she says. She reaches into the cooler and grabs another bottle of pink. "Here. Now you have one for each hand," she howls, cranking off the top before passing it to me. "Drink up, kid."

I don't want to insult Jana, so I finish the orange fizz quickly, then start on the second pink one, just as Eric drifts over. "Having fun?" he asks me.

"You bet," I say with a bit of a wobble. "I've made some new friends. Have you met Jana and Bronwyn and Raiji? They're really nice. And so generous." I giggle.

"Yes, we've met," he says, nodding to them, frowning. Then, quietly to me, "How many drinks have you had, Fiona?"

"Well, I started with a pink one… and now I have a pink one. So I guess that makes one." I snicker again and poke him in the ribs. "You never call me Fiona. Why are you so serious all of a sudden? You're no fun anymore."

I'm starting to feel pretty fuzzy-in-the-head, but I kind of like it. It makes me happy. And giggly. I haven't had a good laugh for a really long time. I need a good laugh.

Eric pulls the bottle out of my hand. "Come on," he says. Still so solemn. "Time to go."

"But my new friends!" I chirp. "Let's stay and have fun with them. We've only been here an hour."

He takes my hand and marches me out of the house. Killjoy.

Then again, it's pretty sweet walking out of a party hand-in-hand with the school hottie.

# Chapter Eleven

The following Friday, there's another party. This time it's in the woods, and this time I don't tell Eric I'm going. He was such a stick-in-the-mud at the last one, dragging me home before ten o'clock. It was so early, my parents weren't even home from Simon and May's house yet.

Eric walked me into the house after last week's party. "What a gentleman," I said, sort of flirting with him. "Damage control," he replied. "In case your parents are here, and you need help explaining where you've been and why you're drunk."

Drunk. Huh. So this is what drunk feels like. I started giggling again. I couldn't stop giggling all night. But Eric wasn't laughing. When he realized nobody was home, he plunked me on a kitchen chair, filled a glass from the tap and handed it to me. "Water, Fiona. Drink lots of water. And go to bed before your parents get back." That's all he said. Stern Eric. I'd never met him before. Then he left, and I was all alone in the house with the dog. Not knowing what else to do, I did what he said. Lots of water and right to bed.

This weekend, I'm not going to do what he says. I actually want to have *fun* at this party. I want to stay out late and drink lots of fizzy drinks. I tell Mom and Dad I'm going to hang out with Tay. What difference does it make? They're going out tonight too, and I'll make sure I get home before they do. That will give me until about midnight.

I head out around eight. It's dark, so I carry a flashlight. But I know the woods so well, I'll have no problem finding the party zone. It takes me about twenty minutes to walk there, a spot pretty much in the middle of the forest. They're not so dumb after all, these party-planners. They picked this spot so that kids from all sides of the forest reserve can walk to it easily. Plus, it's a little off the beaten path.

Even though it's dark, it's easy to find. As I get closer, I just follow the light of the fire. Amy and Charley and the bomb girls are already there when I arrive. I hand Amy ten bucks—

my contribution to the drink fund. I don't know where or how they get the booze, but there's more than one cooler-full just waiting to be consumed.

"Grab a drink and have a seat," yells bomb girl Bronwyn when she sees me approach. I snatch a bottle out of one of the coolers and join her and the others. They're sitting on logs that have been dragged into a circle around the fire. An iPod is attached to portable speakers, so there's music playing. Not so loud that any of the neighbors will call the cops to break up the party, but loud enough to add ambiance.

"Welcome to your first bush bash," cries Amy. "Cheers!" The girls all raise their bottles in a toast to me! They don't care that I'm two years younger. I'm becoming one of them, one of the *in* crowd. I'm feeling pretty pumped at my newfound coolness.

"Hey, jail-baby. I see you escaped from your daddy's ex-con clutches tonight. And you didn't even bring your big boyfriend to protect you." Zak. Why on earth do he and his bonehead buddies get invited to these parties? I don't get it.

"Shut up and give me some smoke, Zak," says Jana. I think she means a cigarette, but what he hands her is a joint. Ah. That's how he gets himself invited. He has the hots for one, or all, of the bomb girls, and they put up with him because he supplies the pot.

Zak squeezes in between Bronwyn and Jana, who takes a drag on the hand-rolled cigarette. She passes it to Bronwyn, who passes it around the circle. I'm wondering what I'll do when it gets to me. I don't want to pollute my lungs, but I don't want to look like a dorky little kid either.

It still has to go through Raiji and Amy and Charley before it's my turn, so I get up and walk, casually of course, over to the cooler to get another drink. As I put the bottle to my lips, Amy yells to me. "Hey, Fi, come back here. You gotta try this." She's holding the joint toward me. What to do? What to do?

Just then, more partiers arrive. It's a group of guys. Everyone's shouting hello and high-fiving each other. Then, in the glow of the firelight, I see Eric. I freeze, hoping he doesn't see me on the other side of the log circle. No such luck. He scowls in my direction and comes over. I'm a bit tipsy already, but I don't feel like giggling right now.

"Why didn't you tell me you were coming to the woods tonight?" he says quietly. "I would have walked over with you."

"I figured you were busy," is the only reply I could come up with. Brilliant.

"What is happening to you, Fiona? You never used to drink. You never used to lie. Are you smoking pot now too? You don't even know what you're getting yourself into with this crowd."

He stomps away before I come up with anything to say. He and his friends are just passing through. They continue on to wherever it is they're going.

I drink my drink and pull another bottle out of the cooler. Beer this time. I've never tried beer before. Turns out that I don't particularly care for it, but I guzzle it down before going back to my pink and orange fizzy coolers. There's lemon in there this time too. I'll try that one later.

Before the night is out, I end up taking my turn with the marijuana joint. I can't avoid it without looking like a total baby. After I take a puff, I rinse my mouth with lemon fizz and do a lot of deep breathing to clear my lungs.

Now that I've proved I'm cool enough to hang with them, I go back to the booze for the rest of the party.

At one point, though, I realize it's getting late, and I have to get home before my parents do. I feel like Cinderella fleeing from the ball before midnight. But I have to get out of there. So I just start walking. I know the way.

A branch slaps me in the head, and I stumble a bit before I get my bearings. Once I'm pointed in the right direction, I'm good to go. I haven't walked far when I hear someone following me. I whip around, shining my flashlight in the direction of the noise. Two faces. Amy and Charley. "You're a bit drunk, Fi," says Amy. "You shouldn't be wandering in the woods by yourself in the dark when you're like this."

I tell them I'm fine, I like walking alone, I know these woods like the back of my hand, go enjoy the party, it's all good. But they insist on walking me home.

On the way, I suddenly want to know about that other party—that party two years ago when my dad got into trouble. They were there. "Not the time to talk about that, Fiona," says Charley. "Let's just get you home."

## Chapter Twelve

I wake up around eleven the next morning with a screaming headache, feeling pretty wrecked. My stomach is all queasy, and it hurts to open my eyes. I roll over, and my stomach heaves into my throat. Gag. I wonder if I have the flu.

At least the house is quiet, so I don't have to listen to Mom and Dad telling each other off for once. That's a nice change. Listening to them would make me feel even worse.

Wait a minute. Why is it so quiet? Why aren't Mom and Dad lecturing each other as usual?

I get up, faster than I should have. The room spins. I freeze until the swirling stops. Water. I need water. I go to the kitchen, fill a glass and hunt for signs of life in the house. Nobody's here. Not even Honey.

"Fiji, is that you?" It's Dad. On the porch. I schlep outside in my pj's and find him sipping his coffee in the sun, Honey on the deck beside him. "It's about time you got up," he winks. "Did you have fun with Tay last night?"

Tay? Oh yeah. I told them I was hanging out with Tay last night. "Yeah. It was good. Where's Mom?" I sit down on Honey's bed beside her and pat her on the head.

"Your mother decided to stay in the city for the weekend."

"I thought you went out together last night to watch Simon's band." Simon is the drummer in a band called the Frontier Blooms. They're actually pretty good for a bunch of old guys.

"We did, Fiji. I met your Mom in town when she got off work. We went to the bar to watch the band. Then she went to Grandma's house for the weekend."

"Why?"

"I don't know. I guess she wanted to spend some time with Grandma."

"You mean she didn't even tell you why she wasn't coming home? You two never talk to each other anymore. You just pick fights. Maybe she's tired of it."

Dad takes a deep breath and looks out over the lawn for a minute without saying anything. "Fiji, it's complicated," he says finally. "Let's just leave it at that."

I groan and lie down beside Honey. The bed smells like wet dog. It makes my stomach lurch. I get up and run into the house, to the bathroom.

Dad runs after me. "Fiji, are you all right?" he shouts through the door as I'm gagging into the toilet.

"I think I have the flu," I say. "I'll be out in a minute."

When I come out of the loo, Dad calls me into the kitchen. He hands me a glass of water and puts his hand on my forehead. "You don't have a fever, Fiji. And you were fine yesterday."

"Well, I'm not fine now," I snap.

"Were you and Tay drinking last night?" he asks suddenly.

"What? No," I say. It's not exactly a lie. Tay wasn't there last night.

"Fiona, precisely what did you two do last night?"

I can't think straight. "Oh, you know, just hung out." I can't come up with a good answer. My head's too fuzzy. Why did Dad ask if I had been drinking? A light goes on in my brain. Maybe this isn't the flu. Maybe this is what a hangover feels like. I've heard of them, but I've never had one. I didn't recognize the symptoms.

Dad is staring at me. "Exactly what did you two do last night, Fiona?"

"I don't know. Nothing. Who cares? I feel crummy. Don't you care about that?"

"Of course I care. I just want to know what's making you feel crummy." He pauses. "I'm going to ask you again. Did you drink alcohol last night?"

"No. Well, maybe a little. I just wanted to try it."

"Where did you get the booze? Who gave it to you? Was it Eric?"

"NO!" I shout. "Eric wasn't even there. Well, he was there, but not until later. And he was mad at me for being there."

"Mad at you for being *where?*"

Oops. Busted. I give up. I don't have the energy to keep lying to him. "I was in the woods. With Amy and her friends." I take a deep breath and sit. I know a lecture is coming. I might as well get comfy.

But Dad doesn't speak. He looks at me with real sadness, then stares at his shoes. This is weirdly worse than if he just yelled at me. After what feels like an hour, he looks up at me.

"I know Amy is your cousin, Fiji. But she's two years older than you, and her friends are not the best people. They are bad news. They get into trouble. They hurt people."

"Well, they're nice to me," I say. "In fact, they're the only people who are nice to me these days. They're the only people who don't judge me because of what *you* did. My other friends aren't even allowed to come over anymore because of *you*. So I had to find some new friends. I fit in with Amy and Charley. We have fun. I haven't had a whole lot of fun for the past two years, you know. What's so bad about that that?"

"What's bad about it is that you're fifteen years old, and you're drinking. And lying to your mom and me."

"*You* drink. *You* party. How can you tell me not to?"

"Fiona, you know I haven't had a drink since…"

"Since that night you were drinking at Uncle David's house? When you were supposed to be chaperoning Amy's party? When Morgan came upstairs and started drinking with you? And you let her? And you *touched* her?"

He flinches when I say that. "That's not what happened," he starts to explain. Again. But before he can say anything else, I run down the hall to my room and shut the door. I fling myself onto my bed and stay there for the rest of the day. Dad lets me go, and leaves me be.

# Chapter Thirteen

Now and then throughout the day, Dad knocks on my door. He wants to know how I'm doing. Am I hungry? Can he get me anything? Do I want the dog for company? What I really want is for him to go away. Everything was better before he got home.

I spend the day dozing, reading, texting, listening to music. I finish a bracelet that I haven't had a chance to work on for weeks. It's actually a pretty good day.

At dinnertime, Dad makes me come out of my room and eat something. I pout about it, but I'm actually really hungry. I haven't eaten all day, and the hangover has finally worn off. He lets me eat in the living room in front of the TV. At one point, he mutes the show I'm watching to tell me I'm grounded. To school and back home for the next two weeks. That's it. No gabbing on the phone. No online chatting. No going out. Especially not with Amy's group.

One thing Dad forgets about— because he's been away so long—is texting. Amy and I have been texting all day. We've come up with a scheme to get me out of the house and to another party tonight.

By eleven o'clock, Dad will be fast asleep on the couch, and I'll be able to sneak out. I'll text Amy when I'm leaving, and she'll get someone to come pick me up.

When it happens, I can't believe how easy it is to trick Dad. I throw Honey some cookies, so she doesn't try to follow me, and I'm out on the street, down the block and in the car with Amy and her friend within minutes. The driver is Miranda. I don't know her at all, and I'm not sure she's completely sober. But she gets us to the party house in one piece.

Tonight, we're partying in the vacant basement suite at a girl named Amber's house. I don't really know Amber. I know she graduated last year, and that she's a bit of a loser, but I don't care. I'm just excited to have fooled Dad, and to be out of the house again.

When I walk in with Amy and Miranda, I see Charley and the bomb girls, along with a few others, older girls

I've never met. I would call this more of a *gathering* than a full-on party. It's a small group, and it's weird that there are no guys. But that means there's no butt-head Zak for once, so it's all good.

Everyone else is pretty trashed by the time I get there, so I have a lot of catching up to do. No time to waste! I've already given Amy my donation for the evening's bevvies. She points me to the tiny kitchen and tells me to have whatever I want.

The fridge is actually pretty empty. I grab a lemon cooler—my new favorite—and join the others. Suddenly, Miranda screams. "I love this song!!" She cranks the music so loud that the house starts shaking. We all get up and dance and sing along, shrieking and laughing.

After a few minutes of this, we hear pounding on the ceiling. Which we ignore. Then, "Amber!" a man's voice yells.

"Turn that crap down. I'm trying to watch a movie."

Amber rolls her eyes as she turns the volume down. "Sorry, sisters," she says. "That's my stepdad. I figured he'd be passed out by now. That's usually what he does on a Saturday night when my mom's out with *the girls*, as she calls her old-lady friends."

It doesn't matter, we tell her, and we go back to drinking and dancing and giggling. We just do it a little more quietly. I chug my cooler and go for another.

Miranda and another girl are in the kitchen drinking. I open the fridge, but other than some juice and fizzy water, it's empty. "No worries, little girl," says Miranda, draining her beer. "There's plenty more booze where the first batch came from. And we know how to get it, don't we, Ashley?" Her friend nods knowingly.

"It works like a charm," Miranda says. "Amber's stepdad is upstairs alone. Drinking. So we know he has booze. One of us goes up and asks him to share his stash with us."

She pauses and focuses her glassy gaze on me for a second. "You know what, kid? *You* should be the one to go upstairs and ask him for it. You're young. You're cute. Plus, you're the only one who's still sober. You'll get away with it."

"He's not going to hand me liquor just because I ask for it," I say.

"He will if he's smarter than that other guy," says Ashley. "Here's what you do, my young friend. You go upstairs. You ask Mr. Stepdad—very sweetly of course—for a bottle of wine and a few beers. If he says no, you pull a Morgan. You tell him that if he doesn't hand it over, you'll tell your parents that he *touched* you—in a private place."

I feel the blood drain from my face. What is she saying? *Pull a Morgan?* Is she talking about Morgan and my dad?

"Then you tell him your parents will call the cops," continues Miranda, "and who will the cops believe? A middle-aged man or a sweet little girl?"

"Miranda, shut up!" Amy has just walked into the kitchen. I look at her, shaking my head.

"Amy, what is she saying? Is that what Morgan did to my dad?" I cry.

"Your dad?" says Ashley. "That was *your* dad?"

"Ashley, shut up!" yells Amy, suddenly sober. "FiFi, come into the living room with me right now."

I don't move. I can't move. "You were there that night, Amy. You knew about this, and you didn't say anything. You let my father—your uncle—rot in jail for a year and a half, just so you could have a drink? So you could get drunk?"

"Fiona…"

I can't speak. I back out of the kitchen, stunned. In the living room, I see Charley holding a can of beer to her lips. Charley, who was also there that night. Charley who has been so nice to me. Charley and Amy. My new friends.

I run outside, fumbling in my pocket for my phone.

"Hello," a groggy voice answers.

"Dad," I wail. "Dad. I'm sorry. I should have believed you."

"Fiji, what's going on?"

"Dad, please come and get me."

## Chapter Fourteen

A lot has happened since that night at Amber's.

Of course I've been grounded. Seriously grounded. As in not-allowed-out-of-the-house-until-the-end-of-the-school-year grounded. That's only two weeks away now, though, so I've almost served my time.

Nothing like the time Dad served for something he didn't do. The good news is that I was able to tell the cops that he truly *was* innocent. I told them what Morgan and those girls—my so-called *friends*—did to him. Not that it matters now. He's already been to jail. But he says that my speaking up has given him a whole different kind of freedom.

It's given me some freedom too. Everyone at school is off my back once and for all. The teachers have stopped asking me how I'm *feeling*. Ms. Shama, I mean *Maria*, has stopped inviting me to come to her office to chat. Serious Shama has left the building. Perky Shama is back.

Even Zak leaves me alone now. Well, not exactly alone. He doesn't bug me about my dad anymore. But he hasn't stopped making fun of my accent in French class. Or my rain hat. Or any other little thing he can come up with. He's so pathetic.

Best of all, Lauren's mom lets her come to my house again. Even though I'm not allowed out, I'm allowed to have friends over. We've been making tons of jewelry, and our online store is almost up and running!

Tay brings Rocky over every day to play in the yard with Honey. And I'm allowed to walk the dogs with Tay, as long as Mom or Dad comes with us. We go to the beach now. I want to stay out of the woods for a while.

I see Amy and Charley at school sometimes, but I want nothing to do with them. I know the cops gave them a good talking to about lying to police and sending an innocent man to jail. They got a warning about public mischief or something like that, and they had to go to the cop shop for a seminar of some sort.

Uncle David and Aunt Helen grounded Amy. I don't know about Charley. But I do know the bomb girls got suspended from school. Because of the whole bomb-scare thing, the cops were harder on them about their role in my dad's arrest. No idea what has happened to Morgan in all this. Don't know. Don't care.

All I care about is that my life is pretty much back to normal. I come home from school every day and hand my cell phone to my dad—another part of being grounded. I do my homework, play with Honey, maybe sit on the porch and have a drink—ice tea or lemonade for me these days, thank you very much.

Things might even be getting better between Mom and Dad. They don't fight *all the time* now. It's taken a few months, but it looks like they're starting to get used to each other again. "One day at a time," Mom says. She still stays at Grandma's some weekends.

Then there's Eric. I mean, really— there's Eric coming up the driveway. I wave. Things are definitely getting back to normal.

# Acknowledgments

Thank you to fellow scribe Alex van Tol for encouraging me to try my hand at fiction, and to the real Madame Pierre for her inspiration and ideas as we walked the dogs in the woods and on the beach every day. Thanks, too, to everyone at Orca for welcoming me into the pod with open arms, and particularly to Andrew Wooldridge for helping to make my transition from nonfiction to fiction an easy evolution.

Diane Dakers is a freelance writer and journalist. She lives in Victoria, British Columbia. *Homecoming* is her first novel.

# orca soundings

For more information on all the books
in the Orca Soundings series, please visit
**www.orcabook.com.**